Typeset in Bernhard Modern.

Printed in Hong Kong

Library of Congress Cataloging-in-Publication Data

Joly, Fanny.

Mr. Fine, Porcupine / by Fanny Joly ; illustrated by Rémi Saillard.

p.cm.

Summary: Shunned because of his sharp quills, a good-natured porcupine is distressed

until he meets someone who shows him that he is lovable, quills and all.

ISBN: 0-8118-1842-X

[1. Porcupines—Fiction. 2. Self-acceptance—Fiction. 3. Stories in rhyme.]

I. Saillard, Remi, ill. II Title.

PZ8.3.J675Mir 1997

[E]—dc21   97-9689   CIP

AC

Distributed in Canada by Raincoast Books

8680 Cambie Street, Vancouver, British Columbia V6P 6M9

10 9 8 7 6 5 4 3 2 1

Chronicle Books

85 Second Street, San Francisco, California 94105

website: www.chronbooks.com

MR. FINE, PORCUPINE

by Fanny Joly

illustrated by Rémi Saillard

chronicle books · san francisco

Hello!

Allow me to introduce myself.
My name is Mr. Fine. Mr. Fine, Porcupine.

Perk up your ears, and take a seat. I have a tale to tell.

A pointed tale about this here porcupine.
Yes, that's me, Mr. Fine.
The tale is divine. It won't take much time.

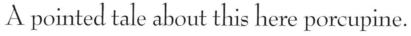

IT IS DIVINE!

Once upon a time, rain or shine,
I'd ride into town on this ten-speed of mine.

Pedal!

Pedal!

Puff!

Puff!

When I'd arrive,
the people would cry,
"Mr. Fine, Mr. Fine!"

"Prickly!
Stickly! Porcupine!"

They'd run,

they'd holler,
they'd scream,

they'd hide.

It seemed no matter how hard I tried
I was a problem porcupine.

You see my quills are TALL and sharp.

They stick straight UP into the sky.

But despite my odd look, I'm really a nice guy.

It's only my hair that doesn't abide.

My hair was a problem,
a problem that grew
and one day when I felt
especially blue . . .

UP

UP

I went to the
park and caused a big
mess (though I never had
thought there would be such dis-
tress). A boy was blowing bubbles
up into the air. I knew that quite
soon they would be in my hair.
He blew bubbles, big
bubbles, and up

UP

up they all flew,
closer **and** **closer**,
if only he knew...

POP!

POP!

POP!

I was always in everyone's way, you see.
I had to do something.
Don't you agree?

What my hair needed
was to flatten, to shrink,
to calm, to smooth,
to lose its kink.

To fix it I'd need lotions,
a fine comb and some spray.
I brushed and I brushed
and I brushed it all day.
But nothing seemed
to work on this big
hair of mine.

Brush!

Brush!

Spray!

Even though I spent so much time.

So the next day I bought a swim cap in a box. I thought it would help by hiding my locks.
Because when you have hair that is so big and F A T

one solution, of course, is to buy a big hat.
No sooner did I put on my new plastic cap, than my hair poked right through …

TAP!

Well I wouldn't give up. I had an idea,

what a hoot!

I'd cover my hair with berries, cherries and fruit!

But down some birds flew....

...right onto my "do!"

The birds ate the berries and gobbled the fruits.

But because of my quills, they lost their feathered suits. (My quills had plucked them downright bare.)

Now I really had to do something with my

big prickly hair!

I could no longer stand to be
different from the rest, causing
trouble, always making a mess.
"Would I forever be alone?
"Would anyone understand me?"
I started to moan.

And then one day
on a whim, on a lark,
I decided to go back
to that very same park.
What do you suppose
I should see with
my eyes, but the

biggest,

the bestest,

the most prickly surprise.

She was picking sticky flowers, and oh, was she fine.
Her hair so tall and prickly—

she was a porcupine!

I couldn't believe my eyes, it was true—
I was not the only one in the world
who looked like I do!

Is it love?

"Your quills are so lovely," she said with a smile.

"Let's sit on this swing and talk for awhile."

Well we talked and we laughed
on that swing at the park
'til the sun had gone down
and the sky became dark.
Then she asked me so sweetly
to be her valentine, and I
responded "Of course my dear,
won't you please be mine?"

TRUE LOVE!

So no matter what
you think is wrong
with your look,
or what style or path
it is that you took …

...it's okay if
your hair is pink,

short,

tall or

blue.

Someone will love you for just being you!

And so ends this prickly story of mine.

Being a porcupine's not bad . . .

IT'S DIVINE!

Especially for me . . . and Mrs. Fine.